Tales of
Robin Hood

Gillian Elias

1994

©Artwork & text by Gillian Elias
for Nottinghamshire County Council

Typeset by David Elias on *DESK*press

ISBN 0 900943 59 9

Contents

Tales of Robin Hood

THE OUTLAWS OF SHERWOOD

In the days of King Richard the Lionheart, the great forest of Sherwood sheltered the most famous outlaw who ever lived. Everyone has heard of Robin Hood, though no one is quite sure of his real name, where his true home was, or how he first came to fall foul of the law and of the powerful Sheriff of Nottingham, forced to hide in the greenwood with a price on his head.

Some people whispered that Robin was of high birth, for he was courteous and gentle, but he was most at ease with the common people, and the longbow, his favourite weapon, was that of the ordinary soldier, for knights were not trained in archery. It was said that Robin Hood was far-travelled, that he had been a Crusader, fighting with the Lionheart's army in the Holy Land. Certainly he loved King Richard well, although in his reign the Saxon people suffered under harsh Norman laws and heavy, unjust taxes. The King was always abroad fighting, while at home his crafty, scheming brother Prince John was plotting mischief. Nottinghamshire was John's favourite hunting-ground, for he had a fine lodge at Clipstone, and was often seen in Sherwood.

When young Robin Hood first entered the leafy glades of Sherwood, many outlaws gathered in the forest, homeless and landless. They poached the King's deer and robbed travellers on forest roads, but they were aimless and unhappy, needing a strong leader to unite a ragged gang of bandits into a brotherhood with pride in themselves and trust in each other. Among them were stouthearted men like tall Will Stutely, a fine bowman, and Much, the brave but ugly-faced miller's son, a renowned deer-stalker, yet there was no natural leader until the sunlit morning when Robin arrived.

The outlaws surrounded the newcomer as he sat quietly on a fallen tree, and when Will Stutely asked who he was and what he wanted in Sherwood, the stranger replied that they could call him Robin Hood, and that he was an outlaw, seeking fellowship with others, ready to earn his keep with the skill of his hands as archer and fighter. His quiet confidence impressed the wary outlaws, always suspicious of strangers, and when Much suggested Robin should show his skill with the bow, he rose with a smile and gathered wild flowers and twigs into a garland. This he gave to Much to hang on the branch of any tree he chose. Deciding to test the newcomer to the utmost, Much selected an oak at a great distance. "He will never reach that mark," muttered the outlaws, but Robin only grinned. Bending his bow with practised ease, he let fly three arrows, and each soared clean through the centre of the garland without so much as touching a single petal.

Will Stutely gazed open-mouthed with wonder. He prided himself on his longbow skills, but had never seen such mastery. Here was indeed an asset to the band! He stepped forward, gave Robin his hand, and welcomed him to the fellowship of the greenwood. The outlaws took him to their hideout, deep in the forest, where they feasted on venison and told Robin of their troubles and adventures, for he inspired their trust, and before long they all agreed that they had found their leader.

THE SHERWOOD CODE

Robin considered the strengths and weaknesses of the outlaw band, and realised that they needed a code of rules to live by, to give them self-respect and to win the loyalty of the local people. He called his men together and told them, very simply, that although they were outlaws in the eyes of men, before God they had to answer for their behaviour, now and always.

Through the heart of Sherwood ran the Great North Road, and along it and a maze of forest paths went hosts of travellers, some with rich purses and fine horses. Robin was well aware that he was captain to a gang of thieves who survived by ambushing those journeying through Sherwood, but he was determined that his outlaws should still be civilised, never offering violence to their victims unless in self-defence, and choosing their targets carefully.

"Never do any harm to a poor labourer, nor any honest yeoman who enters the greenwood," said Robin solemnly, "for as you well know, these men have nothing to spare for the likes of us. If you see a knight or a squire you know to be a good man, and fair to his servants, let him go on his way without hindrance. Above all, for the sake of the Blessed Virgin, never hurt any woman, nor any company which includes a woman, be she noble or humble, young or old. Every child must also be protected. The Sheriff of Nottingham is another story - always watch out for him, as you never know what he might do, and as for these greedy bishops and abbots who live off the fat of the land, you can rob them, tie them up and beat them for all I care, and serve them right, too! Do not be unkind to real pilgrims, though, or to poor priests who do God's work honestly. Lastly, for the sake of your own souls, take pity on the hungry and the ill-used, for if we lose our human kindness we are more like beasts than men."

Robin's short "sermon" was heard in silence, then a buzz of approval went round. The outlaws were decent people who had been driven to seek the safety of the greenwood, and they wanted to be at peace with their own consciences even if they lived by crime.

Robin set about strengthening his band, organising competitions in swordsmanship, archery and fighting with the quarter-staff to keep the men active, fit and cheerful. The hearts of the outlaws lifted, and they soon became known as "Robin Hood's Merry Men" as their leader's fame grew. Many more folk came to Sherwood, seeking to join the company. Robin would test them all by fighting with them himself, and in this way gained his greatest and most loyal friends, whose names live on, forever linked with Robin's own.

LITTLE JOHN

One day Robin was out walking alone in the forest when he came to a narrow wooden bridge over a stream. He stepped onto it, and at the very moment he did so, a huge, curly-haired man stepped on at the other side. Each moved forward, thinking that the other would give way, until they met in the middle of the bridge.

"This is a fine tall fellow," thought Robin to himself. "He must be seven feet high, at least, and he looks strong as a bull. I should like to recruit him to the band if he has courage to match his size."

They stared at each other, challenge in their eyes. "Go back, fellow!" said Robin rudely. "There is no room for two here, and I was first to step onto the bridge."

The tall stranger smiled and said, mildly enough, "Why should I stand aside for you? I have never given way to any man yet, and I see no reason to begin now." He leaned on his quarter-staff, a thick, heavy weapon as long as himself, and his bright eyes twinkled as he looked down at Robin, knowing he wanted a fight.

Quick as lightning, Robin slipped an arrow on his bowstring and drew it to his ear. "Get back now, stranger!" he yelled in pretended rage. "I could send an arrow through your heart before you could strike a single blow at me!"

The stranger's smile did not falter as he faced the archer. "What a coward's trick that would be," he said, "to shoot a man down like a dog, when all he has is his trusty staff!"

Now it was Robin's turn to smile, and he laid aside his bow and quiver of arrows. With his knife, he cut a stout staff of ground oak from a thicket beside the stream, and when he returned the huge stranger was waiting for him on the bridge.

"Let us fight here, where we met," said Robin, "and the man who can knock the other into the water shall be the winner."

"Fair enough," grunted the giant, and the two faced each other on the narrow planking. They whirled their staffs, lunging and parrying, each searching for an opening to get in a blow. Robin ducked under the stranger's guard, striking him across the ribs with a sickening "thwack!", and the giant grew angry at last. He went at Robin furiously, bringing the staff down on his head and almost jolting him into the stream. Now Robin was enraged in his turn, and, shaking the blood out of his eyes, launched himself at his opponent, dealing out blow after blow and forcing him onto the defensive, but without gaining an inch of ground. Suddenly the stranger gathered all his strength and brought down his staff with such force that Robin's oak snapped in two, and Robin fell head first into the water. He came up dripping and gasping, to be greeted by the laughter of the stranger, crying, "Well, Master Bowman, where are you now?"

"By my faith," spluttered Robin, "I am drenched to the bone and well beaten in a fair fight!" Wearily he waded to the bank, pulled himself up, and put his horn to his lips, blowing the three long notes his merry men knew so well. Hardly had the echo died away than the outlaws came running, with Much and Will at their head.

"Robin!" shouted Will. "You're sopping wet! What on earth has been happening?"

"I've been taking a dip in the stream," said Robin cheerfully, "and here stands the man who taught me to dive."

"Let's give the big lout a ducking!" yelled Much, and the outlaws surrounded the giant, ready to hurl him into the water, but Robin quickly stopped them, saying, "Give the man breathing-space, lads! I owe him no grudge, for he fought gallantly. I would rather be his friend than his foe." He turned to the giant and held out his hand. "If you have a mind to try the free forest life, you are welcome to join us. We have need of strong men and true."

"I like you well," said the stranger regretfully, "but I have sworn to follow one man only, and have come to Sherwood to find him. What is your name?"

"I am Robin Hood," said the outlaw, and at his words the stranger gave a great shout, saying, "I have fought and beaten the very man I was seeking! Will you still have me, then?"

"Very gladly," said Robin, warmly. "Men of your size are hard to find, and one look at you is enough to frighten a whole posse of the Sheriff's men! What shall we call you, friend?"

"My name is John Little," announced the giant solemnly, and which the outlaws collapsed with laughter. As soon as he could speak, Will Stutely said, "John Little, I propose you be baptised again, as a newcomer to our band, and Much and I will be your godfathers."

"What name will you give me?" enquired John Little, puzzled and a little offended.

"Why, since you are so small and weak, you shall be John Little no more, but our very own Little John!" smiled Will.

"So be it," said Little John happily, and at the outlaws' camp Robin performed the baptism by pouring a quart of strong ale over the head of the new "baby", after which they feasted on two fat deer, roasted over an open fire. As the shadows danced, Robin and Little John talked together far into the night, for the leader of the outlaws had found his right-hand man to share all his dreams and his adventures.

WILL SCARLET

Soon after Little John arrived in the forest, he and Robin went hunting, for their larder was empty. About noon, the two outlaws spied a herd of deer on the far side of a glade, with a noble stag feeding nearby. They took aim, but suddenly ahead of them a slender young man dressed all in scarlet stepped out from a forest path. The stag, startled by the movement, raised its antlered head, preparing to flee.

"Who can this be?" whispered Robin. "His clothes are too bright for stalking deer. He must be some townsman out for adventure."

But the strange young man had strung his bow, and as the stag bolted he loosed a deadly arrow that dropped the beast in its tracks.

"This is no Nottingham weakling, master," muttered Little John. "That was a noble shot! Give him a suit of Lincoln green instead of that red frippery and he'd make a fine forest man."

"Stay back here, Little John," ordered Robin, "while I talk to this young fellow," and the outlaw quietly approached the man in scarlet, standing over the deer he had killed. "Well shot, stranger!" said Robin, but the young man simply looked at him without reply.

"I am looking for skilled archers," Robin continued, "and I take on all I can. Will you join my men?"

"Who are you?" asked the young man coldly, looking Robin up and down. "Why should I want to join forces with you? You seem to be a forester, by your Lincoln green clothes."

"I am a man of the forest, right enough," agreed Robin.

"You herd deer for the king, do you?" enquired the young man.

"I do indeed - for the King of Sherwood," Robin replied.

"Well, King of England or King of the Forest, I want none of your company," said the stranger. "On your way, forester, and leave me alone."

"And what if I stand my ground?" said Robin, amused.

"Then you must stand a beating," retorted the young man, turning back to examine the stag he had killed. Robin slipped an arrow onto his bowstring and levelled it at the young stranger's head, but he showed no sign of fear, and said merely, "Go away, forester! What on earth are you playing at?"

"I am playing at taking your purse, stranger," said Robin gruffly. "I am no forester, but an outlaw, and young gamecocks like you are worth netting. Throw your purse at my feet or I loose this arrow!"

The young man shrugged and made as if to untie his purse, but quick as a wink whipped an arrow onto his own bowstring, so that the two men, bows drawn, faced each other. "Hold, hold!" cried Robin, impressed by the stranger's courage and agility. "There is no point in killing each other!"

"No point at all," agreed the stranger, "but you started all this, remember."

"So I did, and so I end it," said Robin, taking his arrow from the string. Immediately the stranger did the same, then waited warily. "You carry a sword, stranger," continued Robin, "and so do I. Let us fight before we part, and see who is the better man."

The man in scarlet nodded agreement, so they took their stance on the flat ground beneath the branches of a mighty oak and began their bout. For half an hour their broadswords clashed, metal on metal, in the cut and thrust of equal combat, neither giving an inch until at length the stranger made a lucky lunge and nicked Robin's forehead with the tip of his sword.

Blood began to run down into Robin's eyes so that he could barely see to fight. At this, alarmed for his friend, Little John broke from cover and ran towards the swordsmen. "Give me your sword," he begged Robin, "and I will finish this fight for you!"

"No, Little John," said Robin, wiping his eyes. "This stranger is a fair and gallant fighter who has scorned to press home his advantage while I could not see. I give him the victory with a good will."

"Well," grumbled Little John, "now this young sprig can go back to Nottingham and brag to his friends that he beat Robin Hood at sword play, and lived to tell the tale."

"Did you say Robin Hood?" asked the stranger, eagerly. "Have I fought with Robin himself and never recognised him?"

"Why should you recognise me?" asked Robin, amazed. "Have our paths crossed before?"

"What, Robin, do you not know your own cousin?" laughed the young man. "You used to call me 'Scathlock' when we were boys together!" and he whipped off his feathered cap to show his bright red curls.

"Will Gamwell, as I live and breathe!" exclaimed Robin, delightedly clasping the young man's hand. "But what brings you to Sherwood, Will?"

"I was searching for you, Robin," Will replied, "for I am an outlaw too. My enemies are more powerful than my friends, it seems, and I have run before the Sheriff's men to join your band, if you will have me."

"Very gladly!" said Robin. "Your skill with the bow and the sword make you a prize - and I welcome my good friend and kinsman. Come, Little John, and shake hands with my cousin, Will!"

The giant clasped the hand of Will Gamwell, and laughed, "Like me, Will, you must be christened anew, for in the greenwood an outlaw lays his old name aside!"

"With that red hair and those red clothes, there is only one name to suit you, Will," said Robin. "From today, you are Will Scarlet!"

The three laughing outlaws carried off the stag that Will Scarlet had killed, bearing it away to a feast of celebration, for Robin had found a cousin and the band gained another merry man.

FRIAR TUCK

One glorious summer's day the outlaws went in search of deer, hunting in small groups. Robin's party included Little John, Will Scarlet and Much the Miller's son, and they were well satisfied with their sport, for Will brought down a buck, Much a doe, and Little John a huge hart which he shot from a great distance. Robin applauded this feat by his right-hand man, saying, "Little John, I'd go a hundred miles to find a man to match you with the longbow! Apart from my own good self," he laughed, "I do not think you have an equal!"

Will Scarlet, a little jealous of his rival, quickly said, "Robin, you have no need to trudge a hundred miles! In Fountain Dale there lives a friar who can trounce us all at bowmanship - perhaps he can even match you! And he's a fearsome fighter with sword and quarter-staff as well. They call him the Curtal Friar."

"Is this true?" said Robin, excitedly. "I must see this wonderful friar, and, what's more, I shall go without delay, and before I taste meat or drink again, I shall recruit him to our band. Once we have a friar in our midst we shall be good men as well as merry!"

Back went the outlaws to their camp, armed themselves well, and set out for Fountain Dale and the Friar's cell. As they neared the hermitage, Robin left his men and went on alone until he saw a strange figure pacing by the stream. A broad-shouldered man, built like a wrestler but dressed in a monk's habit, was reading aloud from a holy book. He looked like no friar Robin had ever seen, for his robe was kilted up to the knee, a sword was strapped round his plump waist, and a steel cap sat squarely on his large head.

"This is the fighting friar, right enough," said Robin to himself, "and a tough one, by the look of him," but undaunted, Robin walked on and hailed the friar confidently. "Are you the Curtal Friar?"

"I am," the stout man replied.

"Well, good father," said Robin with a grin, "it seems that if I want to cross this stream I must get my feet wet."

"That's true," said the friar.

"Though if you were to carry me over the water, I should keep my boots dry," continued Robin.

"And what if I should refuse to carry you?" asked the friar.

"Why then, you and I would have to fight," said Robin.

Without another word the friar set down his book, took the outlaw on his broad back, and waded into the stream. On the far bank, Robin sprang down and turned to thank the friar, but found himself in an iron grip and the friar hissed in his ear, "Now, my fine fellow! Carry me back again or it will be the worse for your neck!"

There was nothing for it but to submit, but under the friar's tremendous weight,

Robin kept stumbling on stones and blundering into holes. He managed to struggle across without pitching headlong, and the friar leapt nimbly from his back. However, Robin had thought ahead, and in a trice the friar found a sword point at his throat, as the breathless Robin gasped, "Carry me over the stream again, friar, for my bones are weary!"

Without a word, the stalwart friar hoisted Robin on his back and set off for the third crossing, but in midstream the friar halted, hunched his mighty shoulders, and

dumped Robin head first into the water, shouting, "Now choose, young man, whether to sink or swim!" He plodded back to the bank, laughing, while Robin floundered ashore as best he could, dripping and furious. He snatched up his bow and loosed a quick arrow at the chuckling friar, who caught it neatly on his shield, yelling, "Shoot on, shoot on, fellow!" Robin took the friar at his word and whipped off three more arrows, but, breathless and out of temper, he never so much as grazed the agile monk.

There was nothing for it but the broadsword, so Robin drew his weapon and advanced on the beaming friar, who was still fresh as a daisy. Long and fierce was their battle, the great swords flashing and glittering, but neither gained any advantage, and at last they were forced to pause and lean wearily on their swords. "Give me leave to do one thing, friar," panted Robin.

"What thing is that?" asked the friar, suspiciously.

"Just to blow three blasts on my horn," said Robin.

"If you have breath to spare, then blow away," said the friar carelessly. Robin smiled, knowing what his horn would bring, and put it to his lips. Before the final echo had died away, fifty merry men had answered his well-known call. "What men are these?" asked the astonished friar.

"These are my loyal men, friar," said Robin, "who have come to my aid."

"Ah," said the friar, thoughtfully, "then I must ask your leave in return, to whistle three times."

"Whistle away," smiled Robin confidently. The friar gave three piercing whistles, and at his call fifty great mastiffs came bounding down towards the river. Two laid hold of Robin's jerkin and tore it from his back, and, seeing his plight, his men began to loose a rain of arrows at the dogs, who had been so well-trained that they caught the arrows in their jaws and laid them at the feet of the friar, to the astonishment of the outlaws.

"Call off your dogs, friar," yelled Little John, "for enough is enough, and although I am loth to hurt you or them, I will if I have to, great fighter though you be."

"Who are you?" said the friar, looking with approval at the giant.

"I am Little John, Robin Hood's right-hand man, and one who would rather be friend than foe."

"Well, well! Robin Hood and Little John! Bless my soul!" said the friar, and whistled again. His dogs lay down obediently, the bowmen drew back, and Robin approached the friar, clutching the shreds of his tunic around him.

"What is your name, bold friar," asked Robin, "for you are a man after my own heart?"

"I am Friar Tuck, and for seven years I have lived in Fountain Dale, beating all comers who stand against me."

"Come back with us to Sherwood," coaxed Robin, "and we shall treat you with reverence and build you a church in the greenwood. You will be our priest and confessor, hunt deer with us, drink good wine and ale, and share in our adventures."

"I shall come, and gladly," said the friar, "for I love good company and your souls need saving, for sure!" He laughed heartily, and clapped Robin on the back, packed up his books, whistled his dogs to heel, and set off for Sherwood with a light heart and fifty new friends.

SIR RICHARD OF THE LEE

One summer's day, soon after Friar Tuck joined the outlaws, there was much bustle about the cooking-pots, and Little John told Robin the meal would soon be ready. "Before we eat, we need to find a guest, Little John," said Robin, "a rich baron, or a bishop, or a Norman knight. He can eat to his heart's content - then pay his bill afterwards! Take Much and Will Scarlet with you."

"Very well - whoever dines with us today shall leave Sherwood with a full belly and a lighter purse," promised Little John, and with Much and Will he made for the Great North Road. For a long time the outlaws hid, hot, bored and hungry, watching a deserted road, but just as they were preparing to return empty-handed, a single horseman rode slowly towards them.

He was a sorry sight, and seemed hardly worth stopping, for his dress was plain and worn, his hood drooped over his eyes, and one foot dangled from a broken stirrup. Still, Little John had vowed to bring back a guest, so he stepped forward and knelt before the sorrowful knight, saying courteously, "Welcome to the greenwood, Sir Knight. Come with us, for our master has been waiting your presence at dinner for three hours and more."

"Who is your master?" asked the knight, without much interest.

"Robin Hood," answered Little John.

"I have heard of him," said the sad knight. "People say he is a friend to the poor and needy. I had planned to dine at a wayside inn, but I accept your invitation instead. Lead on!"

As the outlaws led the knight to their camp, Robin, warned of their approach, came forward to welcome their guest with great courtesy. Equally politely, the knight replied, "God save you, Robin, and all your merry men. I am Sir Richard of the Lee." Together they sat down to a magnificent feast of venison, roast swan, pheasant and duck, game pies and pasties, flagons of ale and beakers of wine. The knight ate heartily, for he was indeed hungry, and began to look more cheerful, thanking his host warmly. "I have not eaten so well for three weeks! If ever you come my way, I shall happily repay your hospitality."

"I am obliged to you, Sir Richard," laughed Robin, "but your promise, though sincere, is a poor payment for an excellent dinner. You cannot expect simple yeomen to entertain a knight, so you must put down your purse before you go."

"I will gladly give you all the money I have," said Sir Richard, "but I am ashamed to say it is not nearly enough to pay for all I have enjoyed at your table."

Robin whispered to Little John to search the knight's saddle-bags, then asked loudly, "Well then, Sir Richard, tell me the truth, how much do you have?"

"Only ten shillings, as God is my witness," said the knight ruefully. "The money is in the little coffer slung from my saddle."

"If that is all you have, I shall not touch a penny," said Robin gently, "and if you need more, I shall be glad to lend it to you. Now, Little John, what have you found?" While they spoke, Little John had spread his cloak on the ground and emptied the coffer on to it, and had found exactly ten shillings there.

"Our guest is honest," said Little John, sympathetically.

"Come, then, Sir Richard," said Robin kindly, "take another cup of wine and tell us your story. You are among friends here. Have you lost your fortune? Were you taxed too much? Or perhaps you have managed your estate badly or quarrelled with your neighbours and wasted your money going to the law? What have you done?"

The knight shook his head and sighed deeply. "A man may be ruined through no fault of his own, Robin. Two years ago I had four hundred pounds a year, and now I have nothing but my wife and children."

"How did you lose your fortune?" asked Robin.

"Through my eldest son," said Sir Richard. "At a tournament, though he was a superb jouster, he accidentally killed a knight from a powerful Lancashire family who blamed my son and called him a murderer. To pay lawyers to defend him, I had to mortgage my land to the Abbot of St Mary's, and now I must repay him or lose my estate."

"How much is your debt?" asked Robin.

"Four hundred pounds," sighed Sir Richard. "But I have no money for the Abbot, and I fear I shall be forced to leave England when I cannot pay."

"But will not your friends help you out?" asked Robin anxiously.

"Friends!" exclaimed the knight bitterly. "I had many friends when I had money, but they melted away like snow in May." By now, Little John and Much, both softhearted men, were wiping their eyes and looking at Robin, hoping he would help.

Robin gazed intently at Sir Richard, as if staring into his soul. "Now think, Sir Richard," he said at length, "surely there is one good friend who could offer security on a loan?"

Sadly, Sir Richard shook his head. "My only friend is Mary, Our Saviour's Mother. She has never failed me yet!"

"Well said, Sir Richard!" cried Robin. "Our Lady is the best security any man could have, and dear to all our hearts. Little John, go to our treasury and fetch four hundred pounds - and make sure you count it carefully."

Little John and Will Scarlet rushed to fetch the money, but were so flustered and so sorry for the knight that they brought back five hundred and sixty gold coins. When scolded for poor accounting by Much, Little John was quick to retort, "This good knight has fallen on hard times - he needs a little extra, for his clothes are worn and his horse is tired! A guest of Robin Hood cannot be allowed to go shabbily on his way!"

The other outlaws agreed, and bustled about to find suitable clothes and boots from their store, as well as a strong grey courser for the knight to ride. Robin, laughing, dug out a pair of golden spurs to add the final touch to their gifts, and Sir Richard was close to tears from gratitude and relief. "How can I repay you, my dear friends?" he begged.

"In twelve months, under this same tree, we shall expect to see you again. But wait, Sir Richard!" Robin was struck by a sudden idea. "A noble knight should not ride out alone. Take Little John along as your servant - he'll make a sweet little page to trot at your heels!"

At this the outlaws laughed until they cried, and Sir Richard and his mighty page departed for St Mary's Abbey at once, for by the next sunset the knight had to clear his debt to the Abbot.

SIR RICHARD PAYS HIS DEBT

Next day the Abbot of St Mary's sat feasting with his guest, the corrupt and greedy Chief Justice of England, whom he had bribed to support his shaky claim to Sir Richard's lands. "It is exactly a year since that beggarly knight borrowed four hundred pounds from us, and if he fails to repay, we shall seize his whole inheritance," boasted the Abbot gleefully.

"God help him," said the Prior, a good and holy man. "We would do better to lend him more money than to take all he has. We do not deal charitably with his suffering by foreclosing, and our consciences will surely plague us."

"By heaven and Saint Matthew!" snapped the Abbot peevishly. "Why must you always witter on about charity? This is business!"

At that moment the High Cellarer entered, a huge monk with a fat, ugly face, who rubbed his hands greedily, saying, "Sir Richard has still not come, so St Mary's will shortly possess his whole estate."

They were all still laughing when Sir Richard and Little John rode up to the abbey gate, where the porter greeted them, startled at the splendid horses they were riding. "Welcome, Sir Knight!" he cried. "My Lord Abbot is at dinner with company, and I know they expect your arrival. Let me take your fine mounts to the stable, where we can look after them."

"No," said Sir Richard firmly, "we shall not stay long. Leave them saddled here in the forecourt." He dismounted and strode purposefully into the great hall of the abbey, where the surprised Abbot broke off from devouring a partridge pie. Sir Richard knelt, and spoke politely. "Greetings, my lord Abbot. You see that I have kept my day."

"Yes, I see that," spluttered the Abbot, "but have you brought my money with you?"

"I am here to ask you for more time to pay," said Sir Richard, quietly.

"You miserable debtor!" barked the Abbot. "Not one day more!"

Sir Richard looked towards the Chief Justice. "Surely you, sir, and the Law will help me?"

"I cannot," smirked the official. "You must obey your contract, or your lands are forfeit."

"Then, Lord Abbot," pleaded Sir Richard, "as a Christian, pray extend to me your charity, and hold my lands in trust until I have given your four hundred pounds into your hands!"

But the Abbot merely sneered, "Don't come to me for charity! Unless you pay, your lands are mine."

"By heaven," exclaimed Sir Richard, "it is as well for a man to know who his true friends are, and whose faith is false!"

Ashamed, despite himself, the Abbot took refuge in anger, storming and yelling, "Out of my hall, you false knight!"

Angry in his turn, Sir Richard rose, but with dignity,

and retorted, "In your own hall, Abbot, and before your monks I denounce you. You are no man of God - you have no manners, no breeding and no charity. Your vicious greed is a disgrace to Our Lady and to your Holy Order!"

Even the Chief Justice could see the truth of this, and plucked at the Abbot's sleeve to persuade him to be less grasping, but whilst the Abbot still fumed, Sir Richard stalked up to the table and emptied four hundred gold coins from his leather purse. "Take your gold, Abbot," he said contemptuously. "If you had shown me more courtesy I should have rewarded your Abbey more generously for helping me!"

The Abbot seemed to shrivel in his chair, shocked and ashamed, regretting now the fat fee he had given the Chief Justice to back his claim. To the now silent company, Sir Richard continued, "I have kept my word and my day, and you have no more claim to my lands. I thank God that no grasping Abbot shall be my heir!" With that, he turned on his heel and strode out to where Little John waited with the horses in the courtyard.

Sir Richard told Little John the full story as they rode homeward, happy as larks, but the knight did not linger in the greenwood, being anxious to return to his castle and his waiting lady. She rushed fearfully to meet him at the gate, but her heart filled with joy to see his face alight with gladness. "We have been saved by Robin Hood, dear wife," he cried, "and we must pray for his soul! He has saved us from ruin by lending me enough to pay that greedy Abbot, and we have a full year to work and save enough to pay kind Robin, for I would not fail him for the world!"

ALLAN A'DALE

Robin was walking alone in the forest when he heard a strong, sweet voice singing merrily to a harp. Robin loved music, and was curious about the singer, so he took cover beside the forest path as a young minstrel came into sight. He was handsome, with blond curly hair, and was dressed in scarlet, with a peacock feather in his cap. Robin smiled to himself, realising that the minstrel's bright clothes were part of his performance, though he was almost certainly poor as a church mouse. Whistling the air the young man had sung, Robin slipped away, back to camp and his supper.

Next morning, Robin, Little John and Much were scouting along the same road when the young minstrel happened by again, but sadly changed. In place of his scarlet tunic, he wore black, and though he hugged his harp as he walked, there was no song on his lips. He sighed bitterly as he trudged along, but when Much and Little John suddenly confronted him, the minstrel showed he was no coward and whipped a dagger from his belt to defend himself.

"We mean you no harm, lad," said Little John gently, "but our master would like a word with you. Look, there he stands under that tree!" They led him over to Robin, who greeted him courteously and asked, knowing the likely answer, whether he had any money to spare.

"Very little, I am sorry to say," said the youth, "just five shillings and this ring, and you are welcome to that, though I kept it seven years."

Robin looked at the plain gold band, a wedding ring. "Well, young man, you are sadly altered from your joy of yesterday, so tell us your tale," said Robin.

"Oh, yesterday was yesterday," sighed the young man. "Then I was about to marry a beautiful girl who loves me, but because I am poor, her family have arranged to wed her this day to a rich knight who is old enough to be her grandfather, and my heart is breaking."

Thoughtfully, Robin asked the young man his name, and was told 'Allan A'Dale'. "Well, Allan A'Dale, I am Robin Hood, and I have a mind to help you in your trouble. What will you give me if I can save your true love from this greybeard marriage and return her to your arms?"

At this, Allan began to look hopeful, but the shadow of his penniless state crossed his face again. "I have no money but these few shillings, and you would deserve a fortune for doing me such a favour. All I can offer is myself and my humble, loyal service."

"Allan, I would rather have a loyal man, especially one who can play the harp and sing as sweetly as you can, than a purse of gold. Now, where is this wedding to be?"

"At the church on the edge of the wood, five miles from here," said Allan. "Alice must be already on her way there."

"Then we must lose no time," said Robin. He thought for a moment, then asked Allan to lend him his harp, and went off to the store-cave to change quickly from his Lincoln green into a minstrel's garb. Meanwhile, Little John mustered twenty-four of the best archers, and without delay they sped off for the church.

When they arrived, the outlaws and Allan surrounded the church and hid whilst Robin strolled boldly up the path, harp in hand, twanging the strings as he went. The sound drew to the church door a plump figure in fine robes, the Bishop of Hereford, who was to perform the ceremony, for he and the bridegroom were old friends. "When I heard a harp, I thought the wedding procession was coming," said the Bishop. "Who are you, stranger?"

Robin swept off his feathered cap and bowed low before the Bishop. "Your Grace, I am a wandering harper who heard of this grand wedding and came here to make music."

"Then welcome, friend," smiled the Bishop. "I love harp music most of all. Give me a tune whilst we wait for the bride!"

"Oh no, my lord!" cried Robin hastily. "It would be ill luck to begin the music before the bride appears!"

"Then get ready now," retorted the Bishop, "for here they come!" And indeed, the wedding party could be seen approaching. The wealthy bridegroom was dressed in a richly-embroidered tunic and gown, but his clothes contrasted with his wrinkled, bad-tempered face and skinny limbs knotted with rheumatism. Beside him, in a splendid glittering gown, with pearls woven into her nut-brown hair, walked Allan's true love, Alice, tears streaming unchecked down her lovely face as she was bustled along the path to the church door.

There was a murmur from the people waiting in the church when they saw the unhappy bride, but only Robin was prepared to utter the words that were in the minds of all. "I have seen many a wedding in my life, but never a worse-matched couple!"

"Silence, fellow!" snapped the Bishop. "Play your harp and keep your mouth shut!"

"Oh no, my lord," laughed Robin, "I play the horn far better than the harp!" With that, he whipped his bugle from under his cloak and blew three blasts, at which his merry men burst into the church, with Allan A'Dale closely followed by Friar Tuck and Little John. There was uproar as people saw the outlaws in their Lincoln green, but

Robin blew another blast on his horn, and commanded silence. "Allan A'Dale, this sweet maiden is your true love, I hear?"

"She is indeed, Robin," said Allan, gazing adoringly at Alice.

"Then, if she is willing to marry you, the wedding will continue, but with a change of bridegroom," ordered Robin. "Come, my lord Bishop, marry these two young people who have loved each other for so long."

"I will do no such thing!" blustered the Bishop. "For, you godless outlaw, their names have not been called in church three times, as the law requires."

"Then if you refuse to do your duty as bishop, I shall just have to make a bishop of my own," and Robin seized the Bishop of Hereford, pulled off his mitre and

gold-embroidered cope and tossed them to Little John to wear. When the giant was dressed, he looked so comical that the onlookers began to laugh, for the cope was much too short and the mitre balanced like a toy on his great head. Ignoring the mirth, Little John marched to the pulpit and bellowed the names of Allan and Alice seven times, in case three should not be enough.

Then Friar Tuck stepped forward, robed himself solemnly, and with all the reverence of a priest in the house of God, performed the wedding of the harper and his lady-love as her family and the old knight fumed, helpless under the threat of the outlaws' arrows. As soon as Allan and Alice had been pronounced man and wife, they returned in procession with their outlaw companions to a feast under the trees of Sherwood.

ROBIN AND THE BISHOP OF HEREFORD

Not long after Allan A'Dale's wedding, Robin's spies brought him news that the Bishop of Hereford, with a great retinue, was on his way to Nottingham to stay as a guest of the Sheriff. Robin knew that the Bishop's baggage would be stuffed with money, for he and his men-at-arms had been collecting rents, and they were harsh and ruthless, exacting every last penny, by force if necessary. Robin felt the time had come to give the portly bishop a lesson he would never forget, so he called Little John, Will Scarlet, Will Stutely, Much and Friar Tuck to dress themselves up as shepherds, hiding their Lincoln green under long grey cloaks. They then killed a fat buck and carried it to the roadside, lit a fire and began to roast the deer.

Presently the Bishop came riding by in his splendid robes, with his column of armed men and his sumpter mules, carrying his baggage and treasure. The cleric stared at the shepherds round their fire, and when he saw they were cooking venison, shouted angrily, "You thieving knaves! How dare you peasants have the nerve to kill the king's deer? What are your names?"

"We are only poor shepherds," said Robin, keeping his face hidden from the Bishop. "We work hard all year, tending our sheep, and just for once we decided to treat ourselves to a holiday by tasting the King's finest venison."

"You bold rascals!" roared the Bishop. "The King shall know of this, and surely you will hang for it!"

"Oh, pardon, good Bishop," pleaded Robin humbly. "A man of God should show mercy to the poor. Do not take so many men's lives for the killing of a single deer!"

"No pardon for you, fellow," replied the Bishop. "You must come with me now to face the King's justice!"

The Bishop signalled to his men to seize the shepherds, but before they could lay hold of Robin he set his back against a tree and blew three blasts on his bugle. From behind every bush and tree a man in Lincoln green rose silently, each with an arrow levelled at the Bishop's men, who saw at once that the odds were against them, so turned tail and fled, leaving their master to his fate. The Bishop also tried to make a hasty retreat, but jerked the reins on his palfrey so hard that the poor beast stumbled and pitched him clean out of the saddle. Little John hauled the prelate to his feet and, to frighten him, snarled, "Shall I cut off his head, Robin?"

The Bishop, white as a sheet, realised who had outwitted him. "Oh, have pity, Robin Hood," he gasped, "for if I had known it was you I would have taken another road!"

"I dare say you would," laughed Robin, "but I shall have as much mercy on you as you would have granted my men, so you must come with us to the forest - but as my honoured guest, not as prisoner. We outlaws have better manners than you bishops!"

So the Bishop of Hereford was escorted, very reluctantly, to the outlaws' camp, where a fine dinner was in preparation. Despite his fear, he found he was indeed hungry, so he ate and drank greedily. However, when his appetite was satisfied, the Bishop became anxious to get away, remembering that he was expected in Nottingham. "I must be going," he said nervously to Robin, "so tell me what I owe you for this excellent dinner."

"I know not," said Robin cheerily, "but as the bill must be paid, who do you choose to reckon the amount?"

The Bishop, thinking that a fellow churchman would let him off lightly, picked out Friar Tuck, and began to untie the slender purse at his belt, but the jolly Friar had already spied the bulging leather wallet on the saddle of the Bishop's palfrey. Little John spread out the Bishop's cloak and emptied out a stream of gold from the wallet, exclaiming, "Well, here's enough to pay for a dinner!" and beginning to count the coins.

The total came to three hundred pounds, which Friar Tuck declared a fair price for a dinner, and Robin decided, "We shall give half back to the Bishop's poorest tenants, and the rest we shall store in our treasury against hard times. The good Bishop will return home with a lighter pocket, but richer in experience and well fed indeed!"

Purple with rage at the loss of the money he loved so dearly, the Bishop cursed Robin Hood rudely, but the outlaw leader only laughed, and patted the Bishop consolingly. "Now, now, your grace, a man should be in good heart after such a meal. It is time for music and dancing, not for bitterness. Play us a merry tune, Allan A'Dale, and the Bishop will dance to it!"

"So he shall!" cried Little John, seizing the Bishop by the arm. Robin gripped his other arm, and together they whirled the cleric into a capering dance until he was wheezing and ready to drop, whilst the rest of the outlaws laughed and cheered. At length they hoisted the unsteady Bishop on to his palfrey and pointed him towards Nottingham, jeering after the furious churchman as he reeled off, vowing that he'd have his revenge.

When he reached Nottingham, the Bishop forced the Sheriff to listen over and over to his moans and groans about his lost money and his humiliation by the outlaws. At last, the weary Sheriff agreed to gather a large posse of men to try to capture Robin Hood, and the Bishop insisted on leading the troops. They set off for Sherwood, and almost immediately they entered the trees, one of the Bishop's men caught a glimpse of Robin on a woodland path. Robin instantly realised his danger, and ran like a deer between the trees, knowing that capture meant death.

Even though they had to go round the tangled trees, the horsemen were gaining on Robin when suddenly he came on a tiny tumbledown cottage with its door open. Inside was an old woman at the spinning wheel, and the outlaw gasped to her, "I am Robin Hood, and the Bishop of Hereford and his men are hot on my heels. If they take me, I am a dead man! Will you help me?"

"That I will, Robin," said the old woman readily, "for your men were always good to me. We'll cheat this Bishop, and laugh over it tomorrow. Go into the back room and put on the old skirt and shawl you'll find there, then give me your tunic and cloak of Lincoln green. Hurry now, we have not a moment to lose!"

Even as she spoke, Robin was doing as the quick-witted woman suggested, and he limped away from the cottage in her old cloak, carrying a spindle and thread as she donned his outlaw clothes and waited. Robin passed by the searching men-at-arms, who ignored the hobbling crone when they caught a glimpse of green at the cottage door, and rushed forward to surround the building.

The Bishop ordered his men to storm the cottage, and they quickly returned in triumph, dragging their prisoner cloaked in Lincoln green, clutching a bow and quiver. In high glee at such an easy capture, the men-at-arms slung their captive over a pack-horse and set off on the winding road back to Nottingham.

Meanwhile, as Robin scuttled away, he was spotted by Little John and a group of outlaws. "Look at this ugly old witch!" said the giant, suspiciously. "She moves very fast, though, and is uncommonly tall. Draw your bows, men - something is wrong here!"

"Hold, hold!" cried Robin, throwing back his cloak so that they could see his face. "I am no old woman, but disguised myself to escape the Bishop's men. I fear they will have taken the poor old dame for me, and we shall have to rescue her." Robin sounded his horn to call his merry men together, and they cut quickly through the trees to ambush the posse on their winding path.

The fat Bishop was still gloating over his victory when a hundred bowmen in green suddenly appeared from the trees around him, and his triumph became dismay as the truth began to dawn. "Who is this?" he stammered.

The old woman spoke for the first time since her capture. "Truly, I believe it is Robin Hood!"

"But if this is Robin Hood," faltered the Bishop, "then who might you be?"

"Not the King of Sherwood, that's for sure," chuckled the old woman, her wrinkled face alight with mischief. As they had done before, the Bishop's men turned and fled, and the rest of the posse followed. Much and Will Stutely seized the bridle of the Bishop's fine dapple-grey horse, while Little John gleefully unstrapped the saddle-bag and found it stuffed with money the Bishop had borrowed from the Sheriff to pay the posse for their efforts. Robin freed the old woman from her bonds and pressed fifty silver pennies from the saddle-bag into her hands, kissing her cheek as he did so for saving his life. As for the Bishop, once again he had lost his money and been deserted by his men. The outlaws tied him into his saddle facing backward, giving him the tail for a bridle, and set the dapple-grey cantering back to Nottingham, jeering again at the Bishop, who could only think bitterly of how much he hated bold Robin Hood.

ROBIN HOOD AND THE BUTCHER

After the Bishop of Hereford was sent back to Nottingham in disgrace, the outlaws were left in peace for a while. They hunted, and listened to Allan A'Dale singing beside the camp fire as they mended their equipment and made new arrows, well content with their greenwood life. Soon Robin grew restless, however, and was ready for another adventure, so when he met a cheerful butcher on his way to market in Nottingham, Robin saw a way of entering the town in disguise, and quickly struck a bargain with the tradesman, saying, "I have a great fancy to be a butcher. How much money do you want for your horse and your stock of meat?"

"We-ell," said the butcher slowly, suspecting a trick, "I'd be wanting a good price for them. Shall we say, four marks?" His price was well above the true value of the goods, as he expected the outlaw to haggle.

"Fine!" said Robin, "I'll take them," and he pulled out his purse to press four marks into the surprised butcher's hand. "There's just one other thing," added Robin. "Would you agree to change clothes with me as well? If I'm to act like a butcher, I ought to look like one!"

"Fair enough!" cried the butcher, happy to exchange his working clothes of russet doublet and leather apron for Robin's fine quality tunic of Lincoln green. He went laughing on his way at the antics of the outlaw, well satisfied with his bargain.

So, dressed as a butcher, Robin rode singing through Sherwood on his way to Nottingham market, where he set up his stall among the other sellers of meat. The market began to fill with customers and the real butchers began to cry their bargains out loud, so Robin began to shout too, but in his ignorance about what prices to charge, he was giving as much meat for one penny as the other sellers gave for three.

Buyers soon crowded round his stall, leaving the other butchers puzzled and angry, wondering who this newcomer could be. "We shall be ruined," complained one. "He is taking all our custom!"

"He is some foolish young man newly come into his inheritance who is wasting his money stupidly," thought another.

"Or," said a third, "he has stolen the meat and cares not what price he charges, unless he is some young blade playing butcher to win a bet."

They muttered crossly among themselves that they needed to know more about the stranger who was hurting their trade, and as Robin sold off the last of his stock (a sheep's head which he gave to an old woman for the price of a kiss) one of the butchers came to his stall and invited him to join his fellow tradesmen for dinner. "Gladly," said Robin, smiling. "How could I refuse?"

The butchers trooped off together to the house of the Sheriff, where it was their custom to dine on market days, each paying his own score. The sleek Sheriff sat at the head of the table, encouraging his guests to pass round the wine, which he was selling to them at a handsome profit. Robin proved the life and soul of the party, inviting all to drink at his expense. The Sheriff said little, but thought much as he eyed the young spendthrift.

As the feast ended, the Sheriff took Robin aside and offered him another cup of wine, asking, "I suppose you have your own estate, and a number of fine cattle?"

Robin smilingly accepted the cup, and agreed, "A hundred acres of good free land, and more horned beasts than I can count!"

"Have you a mind to sell, young man?" asked the Sheriff, scenting a chance of a bargain.

Robin pretended to think for a moment, then said awkwardly, "Well, sir, I would not willingly part with such a good property, but I am always short of ready money, so if you could offer me cash on the nail, then perhaps...?"

The Sheriff could hardly believe his luck, but was still cautious. "That sounds very fair, but I should wish to view the property before I purchase it."

"Why, certainly!" replied Robin. "Come with me now, if you will, and if the estate pleases you, I'll ask only four hundred pounds in gold."

"Make it three hundred?" suggested the Sheriff.

Robin hesitated only briefly. "Done!" he cried, slapping the table, and the Sheriff bustled away to saddle his horse before the young butcher could change his mind.

Presently they left the castle, Robin riding the butcher's mare and the Sheriff on his own nag, three hundred gold pieces safely in his saddle-bag. They talked companionably enough as they rode, but as Robin steered them through the edges of Sherwood Forest, the Sheriff grew uneasy. "Heaven keep that scoundrel Robin Hood out of our path," he muttered, as they entered a lonely glade where a herd of deer loomed suddenly out of the evening mists, startling the horses.

"Ah, here are my horned beasts, my Lord Sheriff, come to meet us. How do you like them?" enquired Robin. The Sheriff did not pause to reply, but dug his spurs into his nag's side in an effort to escape the trap. However, Robin caught the bridle with one hand and with the other drew his horn to blow his well-known call. At the first blast the woodland began to fill with green-clad men who surrounded their master and his captive. Will Scarlet was at their head, for Little John and Friar Tuck were about business of their own. "Here is the Lord Sheriff, Will," Robin greeted him, "come to make a bargain and take supper with us."

"Now I know who you are, Robin Hood," snarled the Sheriff, "and no supper will I take with you."

"Certainly I am Robin Hood, and just as certainly we shook hands on a bargain, so put down your money, Sheriff!" said the outlaw leader. "Your supper must be paid for, whether eaten or not!"

So the furious Sheriff was made to hand over the three hundred gold pieces from his saddle-bag, then turn his horse around and start back to Nottingham, sadder, wiser and poorer than when he had set out to cheat the young butcher, who was no butcher at all!

THE SHERIFF AND LITTLE JOHN

The outlaws were laughing by their camp fire at Robin's fooling of the Sheriff when Little John and Friar Tuck returned, and were told the story of the "young butcher". "That was a merry trick to play on the Sheriff," said Little John, "and I have a good mind to play another. Tomorrow there is an archery contest in Nottingham, and the Sheriff will be there, so I shall go along and take part. The Sheriff does not know me, so we shall see what mischief follows!"

"If he does not know you now, he soon will," said Much drily. "Not many folk are seven feet tall!"

"Have a care, Little John," said Robin, suddenly concerned for his friend. "Go in russet to the castle, not in Lincoln green."

"Never fear, Robin, the Sheriff may be a cunning weasel, but I am a wily fox!" And so saying, Little John went off with Will Scarlet to find himself a good disguise from the store cave. Next morning, Little John set out for Nottingham, making for the great square below the castle where the targets had been set. The hardest test of a bowman's skill was the splitting of a peeled willow wand, but Little John practised such feats of archery every day. He stepped up to the mark and split the willow three times out of three, a performance no rival could approach, let alone equal. The Sheriff, judge of the competition, had no hesitation in awarding Little John the prize.

"Well shot!" he cried. "I have never seen such archery! What is your name, my fine fellow? Where do you live?" With a sly smile, Little John told the Sheriff his name was Reynold Greenleaf. He had chosen his alias well, for its meaning was "Fox of the Forest", but the Sheriff had no inkling of that, for he was too intent on persuading the skilful archer to join the Castle guard. He promised a good wage of twenty marks a year, with a horse and his own servant, for a marksman like Reynold Greenleaf was worth paying well. As for Little John, he accepted the offer coolly, thinking that he could enjoy himself in town at the Sheriff's expense, spy on him for Robin, and be the worst bodyguard a master ever had!

The Sheriff's house was very comfortable, and Little John's duties were light, for the Sheriff liked his company, and all went well for a while, until Little John grew weary of town life and longed for the greenwood and the company of his true friends. One day he overslept, and when he woke, found that the Sheriff had gone off hunting without him. So Little John made his way to the buttery, where the food and drink were kept, and asked the butler for some breakfast. The butler, jealous of the giant's popularity, spitefully locked the buttery door, and declared that as breakfast was finished, no more food could be served until the Sheriff returned from his day's hunting.

"But I am very hungry," declared Little John with quiet menace. "Give me my ration of food, or I will surely hurt you."

The butler obstinately refused, but soon wished he had been more obliging, for Little John picked him up, shook him until stars danced before his eyes, then dropped him on the stone-flagged floor. As the butler lay moaning, Little John stepped over him

and burst the buttery door off its hinges with a mighty kick. The shelves inside were laden with good things, and Little John helped himself to a huge slice of venison pasty and half a smoked ham, then a plum pudding and a liberal sample of all the daintiest dishes, washing his feast down with a flagon of canary wine.

As Little John ate his way steadily through the pantry, along came the cook to collect supplies. For a moment he gaped at the groaning butler, still stretched out on the floor, then rushed at Little John and fetched him three hearty smacks that staggered the giant, for the cook was a well-built man and was far from pleased to see his carefully prepared food being devoured. "You great pie-face!" roared the cook. "What a fine servant you are!"

"What a hard hitter you are, master cook!" spluttered Little John, his mouth full of cream tart. "But if you grudge a hungry man his breakfast, I'll have to fight you, just for the exercise!" The pair drew their swords and began to fight up and down the kitchen corridor, but they were so evenly matched that neither could so much as scratch the

other. The bout continued for nearly a full hour, and as they began to tire, Little John exclaimed jovially to his opponent, "I vow, master cook, you are the best swordsman I have met in Nottingham. You are wasted here, a man of your talents. If you can handle a long bow as well as you wield a sword, come back with me to the greenwood, and Robin Hood will welcome you to his band, and give you two new suits of clothes and twenty marks a year!"

"Done!" cried the cook, sheathing his sword and grabbing Little John's hand. "I'm your man!"

"All this exercise has made me hungry again," complained the giant. The cook took the hint, and brought out another venison pasty, fresh white bread and the best wine. The new friends sat and ate together, vowing that they'd both be with Robin Hood before nightfall.

The cook had a sudden idea. "We won't greet the Prince of Sherwood empty-handed, for the Sheriff has a strong-room full of treasure, and I can show you where it is."

"We should be doing our master a kindness in taking it away," agreed Little John solemnly. "We'll save him the worry of looking after it!" With an iron bar they broke through the locks on the Sheriff's treasury, heaping into sacks everything they could carry away, goblets, spoons, silver dishes and four hundred pounds in gold. They chose two stout horses to carry their loot and set off gleefully for Sherwood, where they found Robin and his band under the great oak they called the trysting tree.

Little John greeted his leader heartily. "Good news, Robin! The sheriff sends you, by me, his best wishes, his best cook, and the very best from his treasury!"

"Welcome indeed," chuckled Robin, "though I am sure the Sheriff does not send these gifts willingly!"

"Or knowingly," added Will Scarlet, "for not an hour since I saw the Sheriff's hunting party in Holly Chase."

"Did you now?" mused Little John. "Then as we have the Sheriff's goods and the Sheriff's cook, we might as well have the Sheriff too!" and off he ran into the forest. Soon he spied the Sheriff in his favourite hunting-place, hastened to kneel before him and said humbly, "God save you, master!"

"Reynold Greenleaf! Where have you been all day?" exclaimed the Sheriff.

"In the forest, seeking you," answered Little John, "and I saw a marvellous sight - a splendid hart with a herd of seven score, all as green as grass. I did not dare shoot at them, for they had such sharp antlers I feared they would turn and kill me."

"Green beasts! That must be a sight worth seeing," marvelled the Sheriff. "Can you lead me to them?"

"Indeed I can, my lord," said Little John, "but come with me quietly and alone, so that we may creep up on them unobserved." The Sheriff went trustingly, his tall servant running alongside his horse, until they reached the trysting tree, where Robin was waiting. "Look," cried Little John, "here is the master hart of the herd!" Robin blew three blasts on his horn and at once seven score men in Lincoln green sprang from the bushes, bows levelled. "And here, my Lord Sheriff, is the grass-green herd," he added.

"Devil take you, Reynold Greenleaf! You have betrayed me!" rasped the Sheriff.

"It is your own fault, master," said Little John, unabashed. "You should not have gone off hunting and left me starving at home!"

Robin came forward courteously, and invited the Sheriff to dine. A splendid feast was already set out, beautifully arranged on silver dishes, with great goblets of wonderfully worked silver ready for the wine. The sheriff exclaimed in admiration, but as he began to recognise his own treasures, his appetite for dinner disappeared. "Cheer up, good Sheriff," said Robin. "Your life is in no danger - I spare it for the sake of Little John and for our sovereign lord, King Richard."

Forced to show good grace, the Sheriff ate and drank as heartily as any, but when the meal was over, it was too dark for the outlaws' guest to ride back to Nottingham. Robin ordered that the Sheriff should be helped out of his fur-lined coat, his padded jacket and warm boots, and given instead a simple cloak of Lincoln green. The horrified Sheriff realised he would not lie that night in a soft, warm bed, but wrapped in a thin cloak on the hard ground beneath the trees, like the hardy outlaws. All night he shivered in his breeches and shirt, and when morning came at last he ached in every bone.

"Now you know how we live in the greenwood, Sheriff," said Robin Hood cheerfully.

"You live a harder life than any hermit or wandering friar," grumbled the Sheriff. "For all the gold in merry England, I would not spend another night here."

"But you must live with us for a full year, to teach you how a proud Sheriff may be a free outlaw," Robin said teasingly.

"Robin Hood, I beg you - before I sleep here another cold night, cut off my head and I'll forgive you! For charity's sake, let me leave, and I promise to be the best friend you ever had."

"Very well," said Robin, "but you must swear an oath on my sword that you will never do harm to me or my men, and if you meet any of us, by night or day, you will aid us in any way you can."

The Sheriff cared not what promises he made, for he had no intention of keeping them. Robin knew this, but felt he had punished his enemy enough, so gave him his horse and sent him home to Nottingham, sore, aching, and brooding over his lost treasure as he plotted ways of obtaining revenge.

MAID MARIAN

Robin Hood lived a merry life in the greenwood, but sometimes he would grow sad as he remembered one dear face he thought never to see again. In the days before he was outlawed, Robin had taught the little daughter of his friend and neighbour how to bend the bow, and even how to fight with a sword and a quarter-staff, for Marian was a spirited girl, the despair of her mother, for she preferred riding horses and climbing trees to sitting at home with her embroidery.

While Robin was entertaining the Sheriff of Nottingham as a guest, he did not know that Marian, now grown into a beautiful young woman, was on her way to find him in Sherwood. Times had proved hard for poor Marian, for her parents had died, and she was friendless in the world. She feared she would be forced into a loveless marriage by the harsh Norman baron who owned her village, and she hoped Robin, her childhood friend, would help her for old times' sake. Marian knew that the famous "Prince of Sherwood", though hated by the Sheriff, was loved by the poor, and she was confident he would be kind to her if she could only discover his forest hideaway.

For her journey, Marian rose at dawn and dressed as a boy, to deceive the prying eyes of the baron's informers. She took her longbow and quiver, buckled on her father's old sword, wound her long red hair tightly about her head under a close-fitting cap, and crept away before the villagers stirred, away like the wind to the shelter of Sherwood Forest. Under the shadows of the mighty oaks, Marian searched eagerly for any clue that might lead her to Robin.

It happened that he was much closer than she realised, for that day he was out alone, disguised as a woodman in a russet tunic instead of his usual green. He had been tracking a herd of deer for an hour or more when he spied the slim figure of a handsome lad looking around him with nervous interest. Curious, Robin stopped in the middle of the path and waited for the youth to approach. "Who are you, and what are you doing in Sherwood?" asked the outlaw gruffly.

Marian did not recognise the harsh-voiced stranger as her childhood friend, and though alarmed, faced him bravely. "Stand aside, fellow," she said, as calmly as she could. "My name and business are not your concern, so let me pass. If you do not, I warn you that I am well able to defend myself."

"What a cheeky lad you are," mocked Robin, "with that heavy sword in your belt. Do you think yourself man enough to lift it?"

"It is sharp enough to hurt a lout like you," cried Marian, drawing the glittering blade from its sheath. "Get out of my way!"

But quick as thought the "woodman" drew his own sword from beneath the folds of his mantle, expecting that his lunge would scare the youth into running away. To Robin's surprise, his thrust was deftly turned aside, and the slender youth proved a swift and skilful swordsman. The outlaw held back, not putting out the whole of his own strength, interested to see how well the lad had been taught. As always, Robin admired courage and cleverness, so when Marian's sword point slid over his guard and scratched his cheek, he called

a halt, crying admiringly, "Hold your hand, brave youth! You are a fine swordsman for your age, and fit to come and join Robin Hood's band and live here in Sherwood!"

As he spoke, Marian at last recognised her opponent's voice. "Robin," she breathed, "have I fought you without knowing? And have I hurt you?" Robin was puzzled, for this plucky young fighter now sounded distinctly like a girl, and she continued, "I came here to find you, but never thought to meet you on the way. Do you not know me, Robin?"

For a moment the outlaw looked baffled at the sweet face and large green eyes, then as she pulled off her feathered cap and shook her russet curls loose about her head, his childhood memories came flooding back, and he cried delightedly, "Marian! Can it really be you?"

The old friends sat on a fallen tree as she told him of her troubles and her escape, asking timidly, "Can you find me a place in your band, Robin?"

"I can always make use of a brave lad who can fight," teased Robin, ducking as Marian aimed a cuff at his ear. "Come, we shall look for Alice, the wife of our minstrel, Allan A'Dale, for she will be happy to take you in, and my merry men will welcome you as our Princess of Sherwood."

Hand in hand, Robin and Marian returned to the camp, to the delight of all the outlaws. Little John and Will Stutely went off to hunt for a brace of fine bucks, and they prepared a great feast in honour of Maid Marian's arrival in the greenwood. From that day, Marian played her part in their adventures, and Robin Hood was never lonely at heart again.

SIR RICHARD OF THE LEE REPAYS ROBIN HOOD

Soon after Maid Marian joined Robin in Sherwood, Sir Richard of the Lee made ready to repay his debt of four hundred pounds. The knight's fortunes had prospered as the months passed, and he looked a different man as he journeyed to Sherwood with his escort of a hundred men, dressed in a livery of scarlet and white. The sad knight was sad no more, and sang as he rode, full of gratitude for Robin's help.

On his way to the forest, Sir Richard came to a bridge beside a meadow where a wrestling match was in progress, and he decided that he and his men would rest and watch the sport. There were fine prizes for the winners, a white bull, a horse with a magnificent set of harness, a pair of soft kid gloves, a golden ring and a cask of wine. Such rich rewards had attracted the best wrestlers for many miles around, including a yeoman whom nobody knew, a fine wrestler

who beat all-comers, easily and fairly. The crowd were not pleased that their local favourites had lost, and some attacked the stranger, who could have been badly hurt had not Sir Richard ridden his horse into the mob and raised the yeoman's hand as the winner. Sir Richard then cleverly paid the yeoman five marks for the cask of wine he had just won, and ordered his men to allow the crowd to drink the winner's health, so that hostility began to turn to merriment. That done, Sir Richard continued on his way, glad for Robin Hood's sake that he had saved an honest yeoman from harm.

The brawl at the wrestling match had, however, delayed Sir Richard longer than he had intended, and by three o'clock Robin Hood was still waiting for his guest, and for his dinner. "Surely it is long past the hour for our meal?" pleaded Little John, hungry as always, but Robin was firm that they should wait.

"I fear Our Lady is angry with me that she causes this delay," said Robin. "I shall not eat until we have a guest at table, whoever that guest may be." And he ordered Little John, Will Scarlet and Much to go off to the main road and look for a traveller to join them, either a rich man to pay liberally for his meal, a poor man who needed food, or a minstrel who could sing for his supper.

So the three outlaws, grumbling a little, went in search of a guest, and before long spotted a monk in black robes leading a procession of seven pack-horses, guarded by fifty servants. "Our Lady must have sent this monk with Robin's money," whispered Little John to the others, "for he rides as well-guarded and handsomely mounted as an

archbishop. Courage, lads, and look to your bows. The three of us must trick the fifty of them to bring back this monk for dinner, but remember, Robin is waiting!"

Little John, in his most fearsome manner, then boomed out, "Stop, churlish monk! One step more, and you are a dead man! What do you mean by keeping our master waiting so long for his dinner, and making him so angry?"

"Who is your master?" asked the baffled monk.

"Robin Hood," announced the giant, but the monk was unimpressed. "That thieving rogue!" he scoffed. "I never heard any good of him."

"Liar!" roared Little John. "He is a worthy yeoman of the forest, and as he has invited you to dinner, you must come, willing or no!" Much and Will had said nothing, but held their arrows aimed at the monk's heart. They had no need to shoot, for, hearing the dread name of Robin Hood, and fearing the trees to be full of archers in Lincoln green, most of the monk's escort melted away, leaving only a groom and a pageboy to help lead the pack-horses back to the outlaw's camp. There Robin greeted the monk and presented him with a bowl of fresh water to wash before sitting down to the feast, asking politely what position the monk held, and at which abbey.

"I am no mere monk, but the High Cellarer," said the cleric pompously, "of St Mary's Abbey." At this, Little John and Robin began to laugh, and the puzzled monk glared furiously at them.

Stifling his mirth, Robin began to explain. "You are welcome here, High Cellarer, for the best of reasons. I had been uneasy all day that Our Lady was offended with me, or she would surely have sent me the money to repay a debt of honour."

"But what has this to do with me?" demanded the monk crossly.

"All will soon be clear," said Robin. "I lent a small matter of four hundred pounds to a knight who needed it badly, for a grasping abbot was pressing him. That knight gave Our Lady as his surety, and as you come from Our Lady's abbey, I believe you have been sent to repay me. Tell me honestly, now, how much money do you carry with you?"

"Only twenty marks for the expenses of travel," said the monk, looking shifty. "I swear it on my life."

"If that is truly all you have," said Robin, "I shall not touch a penny, and you shall go freely on your way, but if you have lied, you must forfeit everything!" He motioned to Little John to search the monk's saddle-bags, and in no time at all gold coins were discovered hidden inside a bolt of cloth, and tipped out on the ground. Will Scarlet and Maid Marian counted the hoard, and whispered the total to Robin.

"Did I not tell you?" cried Robin joyfully. "Our Lady is the most faithful of women, for a man could search the whole world and find no better surety than her word. She has sent me double the amount I lent to Sir Richard of the Lee, and on her word I shall gladly lend money in the future too. My compliments to you, High Cellarer, and to the Abbot of St Mary's, for being such true servants to Our Lady!"

The monk looked on, his sour face ugly with rage, for he was powerless to do more than curse silently, having been trapped in a lie. He had no stomach for more of his costly dinner, and rode away from the outlaw camp, glad only that Robin Hood knew nothing of the plans being laid by the Abbot and the Sheriff of Nottingham to plot the downfall of Sir Richard of the Lee.

The High Cellarer had hardly disappeared down the track than Sir Richard came into sight from another direction, greeting Robin and his men courteously as he dismounted. "God save you, Robin Hood, and all your merry men!" he cried. "I pray you are not offended by my late coming, for I stopped on the way to rescue an honest yeoman who was in trouble, for your sake, gentle Robin. But here I am at last, to repay the four hundred pounds you lent me."

Robin smiled, and waved aside the money. "I am pleased that, as I helped you, so you have helped another, Sir Richard, and kept your honour. But your debt is already settled, for Our Lady has sent the High Cellarer of St Mary's to repay me, and it would be a sin to take the money twice over. Come instead and take food and wine with us!"

The outlaws supplied the knight's men with meat and drink, whilst Robin told of the monk's deceit, and Sir Richard laughed until the tears rolled down his cheeks. As the feast ended, the knight beckoned to his servants, who brought forward from the baggage train bundles of a hundred fine longbows, with strings of the best quality, a hundred silver-studded quivers, and a hundred sheaves of arrows, each with sharpened silver tips and flights of peacock feathers. "Here is a small present from myself and my dear lady to you and your men," said Sir Richard, as the outlaws gasped with delight.

"I thank you with all my heart," said Robin with tears in his eyes. "Little John, fetch four hundred pounds from our treasury, and give it with our good wishes to Sir Richard." The knight began to protest, but Robin would not listen. "The monk repaid me far too much, and Our Lady would want me to share the bounty with you! You, sir, have many needs, and our life here is simple. But if you are ever pressed for money again, remember to come first to Robin Hood, and you will not ask in vain!" And the knight and the outlaw drank a toast to each other, the best of friends.

ROBIN HOOD IN NOTTINGHAM

It was Whitsuntide and a bright May morning, but Robin was leaning listlessly against a tree when Little John found him. "You show a sad face for a fair morning, Robin," remarked the giant. "What is the matter?"

"I wish I could go to church, like other Christians," said Robin. "I long to kneel at the altar rail on such a holy day, and surely Our Lady will protect me if I go to mass in Nottingham."

Overhearing the exchange, Much came up to Robin and said, "Take me along, and a dozen others, all well armed. The sneaking enemies who would attack you if they saw you alone will hold off when your friends are with you. Think of sweet Maid Marian, who would tell you, were she here, to protect yourself for her sake." Marian was away from Sherwood at that time, visiting a sick old woman who had been her mother's friend, and Robin was sad partly because he missed her. He was touched by Much's loyalty, but irritated as well, and insisted gruffly that he would take only Little John, to carry his bow.

Little John, who did not like being treated as a servant, retorted, "You can carry your own bow, Robin, and I'll carry mine. On the way we can shoot arrows for pennies to help the road seem shorter!" Robin, cheered by this idea, offered to stake three pennies against each one wagered by Little John, and the pair set off for Nottingham, picking targets to aim at along the way. Little John, always a good shot, found his luck held, and before they reached the city reckoned that his friend owed him sixty pennies. Robin, who had not kept careful count, laughingly disagreed, but the day was sultry and the dispute soon grew hot, until both were out of temper and Little John swore bitterly that he would go not one step further in Robin's company, and turned back to Sherwood.

Robin, knowing he was wrong but too proud to admit it, stalked on alone towards the town and the great church of St Mary, high on a hill. There he offered thanks to Our Lady for his safe arrival, and prayed for a safe return, but, undisguised as he was, the whole congregation could see him plainly as he knelt at the altar, and a certain

black-robed monk with an ugly face recognised him instantly. The High Cellarer, nursing his grudge against the outlaw, slipped out of the church and ordered the town gates to be shut tight as he scurried off to raise the alarm.

The Sheriff lost no time in gathering his guard and hurrying to the church, where they burst in with swords drawn. The congregation scattered, terrified, and Robin suddenly realised how much he missed his faithful Little John. Nevertheless, Robin grasped his sword and launched himself at the Sheriff's men, fighting his way to the door, until his blade snapped against the Sheriff's own shield. Robin flung the sword hilt at his attackers, but without a weapon he was doomed, and was soon overpowered, manacled, and hauled off to a dungeon.

News of Robin's betrayal and capture swiftly reached the outlaw camp, and there was panic among the men, apart from Little John, who calmed them by saying, "You should be ashamed of yourselves, for you know Robin has many times escaped from peril, and with Our Lady's help he will do so again - he has served her faithfully, and she will not let him down. We shall have our revenge on that fat-faced monk, never fear!"

Leaving Will Scarlet and Will Stutely in charge, Little John set off with Much to lie in wait on the London road, knowing that the monk would hasten to tell Prince John of Robin's capture and claim a reward, and indeed it was not long before a black habit came into sight. The outlaws had changed out of their Lincoln green, and the monk was not suspicious when they hailed him and asked about the news from Nottingham. "Is the tale true that Robin Hood is captured?" Little John greeted him. "My friend here was robbed of twenty marks by the knave, and we should be glad to know he has been taken."

The monk rose to the bait. "He robbed me, too, of more than eight hundred pounds, but I have had my revenge! It was thanks to my sharp eye that he was captured, and now I am taking a letter with the good news to Prince John in London."

"May God bless you!" roared Little John. "Come, friend, let us ride with you, for Robin Hood has many rough companions, and the road to London is long and lonely." The monk was thankful for this offer, for he and his page were unprotected on their travel, and he was beginning to regret setting out so hastily. They rode along together for a while, talking pleasantly, until the monk was off his guard. Then, at a deserted turn in the road, Much caught hold of the page while Little John grabbed the monk's bridle and pulled him from his horse.

Scrambling to his feet, the monk pretended to beg for mercy, but at the same moment drew a dagger from his sleeve and struck at Little John, who was prepared for the trick and lashed out with his quarter-staff, sending the blade spinning away. The monk staggered against his terrified horse, who plunged and reared, and lashed out, catching the monk's head an unlucky blow with its hoof, killing him instantly. The terrified page sobbed loudly, and Much tried to console him as the outlaws wondered what to do now.

Little John blew his horn, hoping that other outlaws would hear his call for aid. Luckily Friar Tuck was nearby, and readily took charge of the unhappy page and arranged for the Christian burial of the uncharitable monk, whilst Little John and Much continued towards London with the monk's letter for Prince John.

However, when the two men arrived at the court, they were surprised to be ushered not before the Prince but before King Richard himself, newly returned from the wars. The king studied the letter, and proclaimed, "There is not a yeoman in England I would rather meet than this Robin Hood, but where is the monk who should have brought this message?"

"He died in an accident on the way," said Little John, quite truthfully. The king rewarded the pair with twenty pounds, and ordered them to return to Nottingham, giving them his royal seal to show the Sheriff, with instructions that Robin Hood should be brought to London, alive and unharmed. The delighted outlaws took courteous leave of the king and rode at full speed back to Nottingham, where they found the gates barred.

When Little John called to the porter in his tower, he was told that since Robin Hood's capture, his outlaws had been shooting at the guards on the town walls, so they dared not open the gates. Little John held up the king's seal to show that they were messengers, and they were admitted without more ado, to attend on the Sheriff. Since he had been "Reynold Greenleaf", Little John had shaved off his beard, and he was confident the Sheriff would not recognise him in the guise of a King's Messenger.

At first the Sheriff was

puzzled, asking what had become of the High Cellarer, but Little John thought quickly and claimed that the monk had been made Abbot of Westminster, and hinted that rewards would also be coming the Sheriff's way. The delighted host called for wine and food for his guests, and drank so heartily in celebration that he had to be helped to his bed, leaving Little John and Much free to creep quietly down to the dungeons in the dead of night. There they set up a great noise outside the gaoler's lodging, crying that Robin Hood had broken free and was escaping the castle.

Groggy from sleep, the gaoler stumbled out in alarm, to be greeted by a bear hug from Little John as Much lifted his sword and keys from his belt. The dazed gaoler was quickly locked into a spare cell, and within a few moments Robin had been freed and given the gaoler's sword. Silent now, the three comrades tiptoed out of the castle to the town wall, flung a rope over and clambered down to safety outside. The darkness covered them as they raced away to the greenwood, trying not to laugh out loud as they ran.

It was dawn before the Sheriff, fuddled and lightheaded, realised that Robin had escaped him, and how he had been tricked. Angrily he ordered the town bell to be rung and a great reward to be offered for Robin's recapture, but search as they might through every street and alley, Robin was far beyond the walls and the Sheriff's wrath, feasting happily in Sherwood.

Little John turned to his leader and said, rather sadly, "I have done you a good turn for a bad one, and thanks to me you are here with your merry men, so now I will say goodbye to you, and be on my way."

"Never!" said Robin, with tears in his eyes. "You are the better man. I will stand down and you shall be leader in my stead!"

"Since you say this to me, I am content to serve you still," said Little John. "I did not know you valued me so highly."

The two friends now understood each other better, and were happy that they had made the Sheriff of Nottingham furious. They did not know that King Richard, who at first was also furious, was reluctantly admiring of an outlaw who could command such loyalty, and had become curious to meet the remarkable Robin Hood and his faithful man, Little John, who had made fools of them all.

ROBIN HOOD AND GUY OF GISBORNE

One summer morning, Robin was woken from a strange dream by a bird singing in the lime trees. He was troubled and uneasy in his mind, and over breakfast he described his dream to Little John. "Two strong men overcame me and beat me, bound me with rope and took away my bow. I shall keep a sharp look-out for that pair, as sure as my name is Robin Hood."

"Dreams are neither here nor there, Robin," advised Little John. "They are like winter gales in the forest - loud in the night, but forgotten in the morning."

But Robin was still uneasy. "The dream felt like a warning, and I must search the glades in case these two fellows are in the forest. Will you come with me?"

Sighing at Robin's strange mood, the giant agreed, and the friends prowled the woodland for over an hour before they spied a strange figure leaning against a tree. He was tall and strongly-built, dressed from head to foot in a horse hide, complete with mane and tail. He looked a dangerous man, with sword and dagger strapped to his side. Ever protective of his leader, Little John whispered, "Wait here, Robin. Let me find out what this odd fellow wants in Sherwood!"

But Robin would not hang back, and snapped, "What kind of chief do you think I am? When did I ever send another into danger instead of me? If I were not afraid of snapping my longbow, I'd crack your thick head with it!" Little John suddenly lost patience with Robin's quarrelsome mood, taking the hasty words too much to heart, and stalked off, leaving Robin to do what he would.

Little John slipped swiftly through the trees, his anger cooling as he scouted for traces of deer, and he was beginning to feel he had been too impulsive when he heard a cry of one of his friends in trouble. Ahead he could see two of the outlaws lying wounded on the grass, while Will Scarlet was running like a hare with the Sheriff's men in hot pursuit.

Hastily, Little John loosed an arrow at one swift runner who was on Will's heels, but as he fired, the great bow cracked, leaving the giant outlaw with no weapon, facing an onrush of enemies. The arrow from the broken bow flew straight, however, and brought down the Sheriff's man, as Will Scarlet vanished into a thicket. Little John was not so lucky, and was overpowered and bound by five grinning men-at-arms, then hauled before the waiting Sheriff.

This time, the Sheriff recognised "Reynold Greenleaf", against whom he bore such a grudge, and once he was satisfied the giant was safely bound, began to gloat. "You'll be dragged from here to the gallows, you rogue, then hanged high for all the people of Nottingham to see!"

"If it is God's will," said Little John quietly. "You may fail." The Sheriff merely smirked, and ordered his men to guard their captive well.

Meanwhile, Robin had walked boldly up to the stranger wearing the horse's hide, and greeted him cheerfully. "Good day, neighbour! I see from your bow that you are a fellow archer. Do you come to hunt?" The man did not return Robin's greeting, but muttered that he had lost his way, and gazed around him, frowning. "I will lead you through the forest," offered Robin. "I promise you could have no better guide."

"I am looking for an outlaw," said the stranger, abruptly. "Can you lead me to the man they call Robin Hood? I should rather meet him than have a purse full of gold."

"No doubt he will be pleased to meet you, too," said Robin carefully. "Let us sport a little with our arrows as we seek him, and perhaps you will come upon Robin Hood when you least expect it." Reluctantly the stranger agreed to this proposal, and the two cut slender wands and wove garlands from the summer greenery to make targets, which they set three hundred paces away.

They shot in turn, and Robin's first arrow missed his target by less than an inch. The stranger, though a powerful bowman, shot high, and though his next arrow caught the edge of the garland, Robin's second shot split the willow wand in the very centre. The stranger was greatly impressed. "Bless my heart! You are a wonderful shot, better than the famed Robin Hood himself! Tell me your name, fellow!"

"I shall, when I know who asks," Robin replied.

"I am Guy of Gisborne, a dangerous man to know, as Robin Hood will find to his cost, for I have taken the Sheriff's gold and sworn to bring the outlaw back to Nottingham."

Robin laughed. "Indeed! I am Robin Hood of Sherwood, and I too am a dangerous fellow to know. I care nothing for the Sheriff, and even less for you, Guy of Gisborne!"

At this, the fearsome Guy of Gisborne drew his sword, and in the heat of the summer day, the outlaw and the Sheriff's man fought relentlessly, around the glade and between the trees, until Robin stumbled on a root and was caught in the side by Gisborne's blade. He fell against a tree, badly hurt, but in his pain called upon the Blessed Virgin, crying, "Dear Lady, Mother and Maiden! Help me now, for it was never a man's fate to die before his time!" Then, summoning all his fading strength, he leaped aside as his opponent lunged triumphantly at him, and took Guy of Gisborne fatally in the neck with a high backward cut. Weak and breathless, Robin stood over the body of his mercenary foe, and thought to himself, "You were a traitor to honest yeomen all your days, but now your time is over."

Robin unstrapped the horse-hide from Gisborne's body, and in its place draped his own green mantle. With an inward shudder, he dressed himself in the hide, took Gisborne's sword, bow, and hunting-horn, and went in search of his outlaw band. As he neared their camp, however, he saw the Sheriff ahead, glaring triumphantly at the captive Little John, so he slipped back into the cover of the trees and thought rapidly. He then put Guy of Gisborne's horn to his lips and blew loudly, to the great delight of the Sheriff, who cried, "I hear nothing but good news! That is the bugle of Guy of Gisborne, who must have vanquished Robin Hood!"

At that moment, Robin stepped into view, and the Sheriff, recognising the horse-hide, rushed forward to greet the blood-stained figure. "Here is my worthy champion! Welcome, Guy of Gisborne - you may ask whatever you want of me for this deed!"

Robin kept his face hidden in the folds of the horse-hide, and mumbled, "I do not seek your gold, Sheriff, but what I have done for the master I would seek to do for his man also. I ask only that I should be famed far and wide for dispatching both Robin Hood and his giant friend!" He pointed to Little John, who had quickly recognised Robin's voice, and knew that his chance to escape was close at hand.

The greedy Sheriff was quick to agree the terms, thinking Little John a good exchange for a golden payment, and Robin strode over to the giant, commanding his guards, "Stand back! Give me space to swing freely at this giant!" as he whirled his sword. The soldiers backed respectfully away, a quick flash of a blade sliced through Little John's bonds, and Robin thrust Guy of Gisborne's bow into the giant's hands.

When the Sheriff saw Little John bend the bow, he whisked his horse around to make off at high speed back to Nottingham, and as outlaws, alarmed by the blast on Guy's horn, began to make their way to the spot, the Sheriff's men were close behind their cowardly master. Happy and grateful for his rescue, Little John helped his leader, faint and still bleeding from his wound, back to their camp to recover.

THE SILVER ARROW

The Sheriff of Nottingham sat at home, brooding bitterly over how Robin Hood had escaped so often from his clutches, and made him look foolish in the eyes of the king. "If I cannot take this rascal by force," he said to himself, "I must try cunning instead. Above all things, Robin prides himself on his skill as an archer, so I shall proclaim a great tournament to lure this so-called Prince of Sherwood with an irresistible prize! But what shall it be? Ah, I have it - a precious arrow, with a shaft of pure silver and a tip and flight of rich, red gold! That will draw him from his hideout into my clutches!"

Robin had been cruelly wounded in his fight with Guy of Gisborne, and it took all Marian's devoted care and Friar Tuck's herbal skills to bring back his strength. Through the long summer he had rested, but with the crisp autumn days, Robin was well again, ready for another adventure. When Much brought news of the Sheriff's tournament, Robin decided at once that he must compete, if only to snatch the coveted prize from under the Sheriff's bony nose. "My merry men are the best archers in England," he said gleefully, "and we shall bear away all the prizes!"

But Marian shook her bright curls doubtfully. "Do not go, dear Robin," she pleaded. "I am sure this is some trick by the Sheriff to draw you into his power, for he knows the silver arrow will tempt you from the forest."

Little John, who had great respect for Marian's opinions, but who also longed to show off his skills with the longbow, had a clever suggestion. "We should be able to outwit the Sheriff if we break into small groups, mixing with the crowds at the tournament but staying always within bugle call. No shred of Lincoln green, either - we must dress in ordinary country clothes, and you and I, Robin, are too well known, so we must disguise our faces. My height I cannot disguise, but there will be other tall yeomen there, and I shall try to blend in with the rest."

"I am still worried about all this," said Marian, only half persuaded, "but if you must go, I shall come too, dressed as Friar Tuck's page!"

The outlaws ransacked their stores for clothes and disguises, and when all was ready they set off for Nottingham in groups of four or five by roundabout routes. The archery butts on Castle Green were long and well laid out, and the Sheriff stood on a platform nearby, raking the crowd of archers with hungry eyes for a glimpse of his arch-enemy. Robin had chosen for his team Little John, Will Scarlet, Much, Will Stutely and a new member of his band, Gilbert of the White Hand, a very fine archer. His band were the last to shoot, and all aimed well, but Robin, in his red jacket, split the willow

wand with each of his three arrows, and the crowd roared their appreciation of his skill.

"Not even Robin Hood could shoot so well," said one merchant to the Sheriff.

"Yes," replied the Sheriff, "I had hoped to find Robin Hood here today, but as you see, he has not dared come to Nottingham." Overhearing this exchange, Robin smiled to himself, then went forward to receive his prize. As he bowed, and stretched out his hand for the silver arrow, the Sheriff suddenly saw through his disguise, but hesitated for a fatal moment, allowing Robin to take his trophy and bound away to the edge of the enclosure, outlaws streaming towards him from all directions.

Then two shrill blasts of a trumpet summoned the Sheriff's armed men, and the outlaws knew they would have to fight their way home to the greenwood. Friar Tuck defended Marian, while Robin and his chief men plunged, bows at the ready, into the thick of the fighting. The outlaws shot so fiercely and truly that the Sheriff's men could not get near to Robin, and they soon fled to save their own skins. As the soldiers broke, the outlaws reached the town gate and retreated towards the greenwood with a scatter of arrows pursuing them from the castle walls.

By ill luck, one arrow caught Little John in the leg, and he fell heavily. "Robin!" he gasped. "If you ever loved me, kill me now. Do not let the Sheriff take me alive!"

"Your life is worth more to me than all the gold in merry England," cried Robin, kneeling beside his friend. Then Much ran up, and hoisted the giant on his broad shoulders, saying, "God forbid we should leave you behind, Little John!" Robin and the others held off their pursuers with arrows as Much struggled under his heavy burden, and so the outlaws toiled on until they came to a castle with a high wall and a moat.

"Thanks be to Our Lady!" breathed Robin in relief. "This is the home of Sir Richard of the Lee," and no sooner had he spoken than the gate opened wide and Sir Richard welcomed them all inside.

"There is no-one in the whole world I honour more than you, Robin," said the knight. "You will all be safe here from the Sheriff!" He ordered his men to raise the drawbridge and man the walls, then drew his guests inside the castle. Wounds were tended and soothed, food was brought, and the outlaws rested, safe in the home of their friend.

Meanwhile, the Sheriff had been told of the outlaws' refuge and had brought reinforcements to surround Sir Richard's castle. When the knight appeared on the ramparts, the Sheriff called out to him, "You traitor knight! You are sheltering the king's enemies in defiance of the law!"

Sir Richard was undismayed. "I shall stand by what I have done, as a true knight," he declared. "Go away and trouble me no more until you know the king's will in this matter!"

The Sheriff decided to act on this advice, and rushed off to London at once, pouring out his complaints against Robin Hood and his champion, Sir Richard of the Lee, pointing out that the knight was defying the king's own authority.

The king was, as ever, calm and stern, saying, "I shall come to Nottingham in two weeks, and shall take this knight and Robin Hood too. Go home, Sheriff, and gather as many good bowmen as you may." So the Sheriff took his leave of King Richard, but when he reached Nottingham he found, much to his rage, that Robin and his men had left the castle and returned to Sherwood, as had Little John, whose wound was healing. Since the outlaws had escaped him, the Sheriff was determined to seize the knight, and when Sir Richard rode out of his castle to go hawking, he was captured by the Sheriff's men, shackled with chains, and marched off towards Nottingham.

Sir Richard's lady was as brave as she was beautiful, and when she heard that her husband had been seized, rode off alone into the heart of Sherwood to find Robin. Will Scarlet saw her white palfrey galloping headlong down a forest path, and led her to the outlaws' camp, where she gasped out her news, crying, "For the sake of the Blessed Virgin, come to our aid! Do not let my husband be shamefully put to death by the Sheriff. At this very moment he is being taken to Nottingham, and all for your sake! Oh, hurry, Robin, they are not yet three miles on their way!"

"Never fear, Lady!" said Robin. "We shall bring Sir Richard home safely to you. To arms, my merry men! I have need of you all!" The whole camp sprang into action at once, some mounted, some running as fast as they could on a mad chase towards Nottingham. They were in time to hide among the trees and bushes beside the highway before the procession came into sight, with Sir Richard stumbling along beside the Sheriff's horse.

"Bide your time, men," commanded Robin. "Take aim and be ready, but leave the Sheriff to me!" Then he called out, "Stand, traitor Sheriff! I want a word with you! It is seven years since I travelled so fast as I have today, and you shall suffer for it. Move away from your prisoner, for I have a score of arrows aimed at your heart, and not a soul but you will suffer a moment's pang if that heart stops beating!"

At Robin's words, like green shadows, the bowmen appeared from the trees and took aim. As they had done many a time before, the Sheriff's men took to their heels and headed for the town gates, clamouring to be let in, and the Sheriff was not slow to follow them. Much darted forward to free Sir Richard, and the outlaws, surrounding him like a living shield, brought him safely back to the greenwood, and the arms of his loving wife. Sir Richard and his lady were now outlaws too, and their only home was the forest until such time as King Richard pardoned the knight who had befriended Robin Hood and his merry men.

KING RICHARD IN SHERWOOD

True to his promise, King Richard rode into Nottingham with a grand company of knights, intending to seize Sir Richard of the Lee and his friend Robin Hood. The king made many enquiries about them both, and took possession of the knight's estates. He was very angry when he saw how the numbers of deer had fallen in the forest, and swore than he would make Robin answer for his crimes, but though he ordered the whole countryside to be scoured, no trace of the merry men could be found.

The king knew full well that the outlaws still hid in Sherwood, killing the deer exactly as they pleased. At last a clever forester offered the king some good advice. "My liege, if you want to find Robin Hood, I can tell you what to do. Take five of your best men and disguise yourselves as monks. I shall set you on the right path, and, if I know Robin, he will come to you of his own accord." The king immediately saw the good sense of this scheme, and lost no time in borrowing a set of monks'

habits from an abbey nearby, dressing himself as an abbot, caped and hooded, with a great cross on his chest. Well-laden pack horses followed the company, tempting the outlaws to waylay them.

Sure enough, they had travelled only a mile into the forest when their way was suddenly barred by none other than Robin himself, leading a group of archers. Robin stepped up to the king's horse and took the bridle in his hand, saying, "My Lord Abbot, by your leave, you must rest here for a while. We are yeomen of this forest, with nothing to live on but the meat of the king's deer, yet you have rents and lands and stores of gold. Give us some of your money, for holy charity."

The king answered mildly, saying, "I have only forty pounds

with me, for I have been in Nottingham with the king for two weeks, and have spent huge sums entertaining great people. If I had a hundred gold coins I would hand them over freely, but this is all I have," and he offered his purse.

Seeing that this was the truth, Robin gave twenty pounds to his men and, with a low bow, returned the other twenty to the king, saying, "Keep this for your own needs. I am sure we shall meet again."

"Thank you," said the king, surprised at the outlaw's good manners, "but if you are Robin Hood, I have a message for you from King Richard, who sends you his seal and invites you to Nottingham to dine with him."

Robin sank down on his knee at these words, replying, "I love no man in all the world so much as King Richard, and you are welcome, Lord Abbot, for bringing me this news. Come and dine with me under my trysting tree." He led the party to his camp, where a feast was prepared in honour of the courteous abbot and his monks. When the meal was ready, Robin blew his horn, and his men immediately came and knelt before him in obedience. At the sight of such devotion, King Richard was sad, thinking that the Prince of Sherwood inspired far greater loyalty than he did himself.

A splendid dinner was served, with venison and game birds, white bread, red wine and brown ale. Robin and Little John served the guests with all the best delicacies, and when their appetites failed, Robin proposed the health of King Richard and commanded his men to entertain them with a display of their skills. The king protested, when he saw the distance of the archery targets, that the bowmen would never hit their marks, but the outlaws only smiled. "Whoever shoots outside the garland loses his bow and arrows to the winner," said Robin, "and he will also receive a smack on the head! No one is excused."

Robin hit those who lost to him very hard indeed, so Little John and Will Scarlet got a hearty thump apiece, but at last Robin's own shot fell short, and he lost to Gilbert of the White Hand, who insisted that his chief take his punishment like everyone else. "Well, it can't be helped," said Robin cheerfully, "so I shall submit myself to you, Father Abbot!"

"You must excuse me, Robin Hood," said the king, "for it would not be proper for a man of God to strike a good yeoman."

"Never fear, Father Abbot," grinned

Robin, "you have my permission!" At this the king smiled, rolled back his sleeve, and fetched Robin such a blow that it knocked him flat. "By heaven, you are a mighty monk," said Robin ruefully as he picked himself up from the grass. He looked straight into the eyes of King Richard, and suddenly knew him for who he was. Robin fell to his knees, as did Sir Richard of the Lee, who had had his own suspicions about the identity of the "Abbot", and all the merry men, who had fallen silent, and gazed in awe as their sovereign set aside his monk's robe to stand before them in his coat of mail. "My king, I

ask you now for mercy for me and all my merry men, and for this good knight, Sir Richard of the Lee, who has lost all he owned for my sake, and who is a true knight and loyal subject of Your Majesty."

The king said not a word, but looked long at Robin, Sir Richard and all that fair company, and his eyes twinkled as they met those of Little John. Then he smiled and said, "Before God, I grant your pardon, one and all, but you must leave this greenwood and come to live with me in London."

Now Robin said nothing, but gazed at Little John, Much, Will Scarlet, Friar Tuck and lastly at his beloved Marian, then answered slowly, "It shall be so, my liege. I shall come to court and will serve you well, and so shall one hundred and forty-three of my merry men. But," he added, laughing, "if the life does not suit us, we shall be off back to Sherwood to hunt the deer!"

"No wonder you are called Bold Robin Hood!" said the king. "You have a merry life here, and I have a mind to sample it myself. Have you any spare suits of Lincoln green to fit my merry men and me?"

"We have plenty of good clothes, your majesty, fit for a king in Sherwood," said Robin, and led the royal party to the cave, where he kitted them all out as men of the forest, and handed them bows and quivers of arrows. Then, a green-clad army, the king and his knights, Robin and all his merry men left the glades of Sherwood, and were presently riding and swarming through the streets of Nottingham.

At first the townspeople took fright at this invasion, thinking that the king was dead and that Bold Robin had come in force to take on the Sheriff in his castle. Seeing the panic, the king laughed heartily and made himself known, to the great relief of the people who crowded around the king's horse as with his escort of former outlaws he rode up to the castle gatehouse. The Sheriff showed a sour face as he waited for the king, seeing him favour Robin Hood, but he could do nothing.

That night there was great feasting in Nottingham, and at the height of the revels, the king showed his trust in Sir Richard of the Lee, restoring his lands and adding to them, so that the Sheriff bit his lip in fury, and the Bishop of Hereford's face went as purple as his robes.

Before the company left for London, there was a quiet wedding in the little church of Saint Mary at Edwinstowe, in the heart of Sherwood, where Maid Marian became Robin's bride. King Richard himself honoured them by his presence, Little John was Robin's best man, and Friar Tuck performed the ceremony. Then, with sadness in their hearts, the company took horse for London, leaving the greenwood, as they thought, for ever.

ROBIN'S RETURN

For a time, Robin Hood and his people were contented enough in the king's service, but they grew homesick for Sherwood, and one by one the merry men left the streets of London for the well-loved forest glades, until only Little John and Will Scarlet remained with Robin and Marian. Life at court was expensive, and money soon melted away, so that Robin's longing to return home grew stronger each day. One morning, watching a group of young men practising with the bow, he could suddenly bear the inactivity no more, thinking, "Once I was the best bowman in England, and I was free. Now I am a city dweller with an empty purse, and if I linger here I shall die of despair!"

When he found that Marian, Little John and Will all felt the same, Robin resolved to ask King Richard's leave to go back to Sherwood for a time. They knew that the king, who loved their company well, would be reluctant to lose them, so Robin approached him carefully. "Your Majesty," he began, "grant me this favour, I beg. On the edge of Sherwood I built a small chapel dedicated to Saint Mary Magdalene, and I have a great longing to pray there once more. My need is so strong I can neither eat nor sleep."

"Very well," said the king, a good Christian who respected piety in others, "you and your people have leave of absence for a week, but no longer! You must return after seven days without fail." Joyfully, Robin thanked King Richard, took his leave with sweet courtesy, and hurried away to tell the others and to make preparations for a speedy departure.

Robin re-entered Sherwood on a clear bright morning, loud with birdsong. With a contented sigh, he breathed the pure air of the greenwood, then he and Little John spotted a handsome buck within arrow-shot, and all the delight of their old life flooded back to their hearts. Robin put his horn to his lips and blew his familiar call, and at the sound his men, who had not

been so merry without their chief, rushed headlong towards the sound, crying out their welcome. They celebrated the homecoming with a great feast, and it was indeed a true coming home, for Robin was lost to the king's service as soon as he came into his old Sherwood haunts again.

Time passed, and King Richard returned to his foreign wars, only to die in France, leaving his wicked brother King John to rule England, so that Robin and his men were outlaws once more, living on in Sherwood for over twenty years, happy and free.

But time leaves marks upon us all, even upon Bold Robin Hood. When he lost his beloved Marian in the dark days of one hard winter, Robin's strength and joy failed with her, and he fell ill of a low fever, so that the faithful Little John feared for his master's life. Robin was determined to regain his health, for the sake of his men, so he thought of his cousin, the Prioress of Kirklees, who was skilled in the healing arts. In those days, to cure a fever, a patient was cut, and his blood allowed to flow freely for a time. The Prioress knew how to do this, and Robin believed she could do him good.

With painful slowness, Little John helped Robin to Kirklees, stopping often on the way, for Robin was sick and faint, and they were welcomed by the Prioress herself, who had spied their approach from her window. "Cousin Robin," she said sweetly, "how pale and sad you look! I am glad you come to me for help, and you must be bled at once."

Little John carried Robin to a small private room, high in a tower in a deserted part of the nunnery. Once Robin was laid in his bed, the Prioress ordered Little John away, insisting that her cousin needed to be quiet. She opened a vein in Robin's arm and let the blood run free, but then, instead of binding his wound firmly, she left the vein to bleed, and, chuckling to herself, crept away, locking the door behind her. Robin had thought the Prioress to be a friend as well as kinswoman, but for many years she had hated him in secret, and took delight in the chance to do him harm.

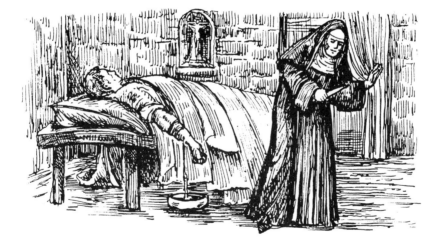

At length, Robin revived a little, and knew that he had been deserted and betrayed. Dragging himself to the window, he raised his horn to his parched lips and blew a feeble note. The anxious Little John was waiting at a nearby gate, troubled at his abrupt dismissal from his master's side. He heard the horn and rushed to the tower, and when he found the door locked fast, charged at it with his strong shoulder. The lock could not resist the giant's strength, but as he entered he realised with a cold dread that his master was dying, and in his anger swore that he would burn Kirklees Priory to the ground.

"No," whispered Robin, "I forbid it with my last breath. I never harmed a woman in my life, and will not do so now. Give me my bow, Little John, and help me to the window to shoot one final time. Where the arrow falls, there make my grave - bury me there, and lay my bow beside me."

Weeping, Little John held Robin as he bent his bow, then knelt beside the bed as the Prince of Sherwood's spirit passed from his body. He marked where the arrow fell, beside a yew tree, and took a spade from the Priory garden to dig the grave where he laid his master tenderly, wrapped in his mantle of Lincoln green, his longbow at his side. Blowing one last long note on Robin's horn, Little John placed that on Robin's breast, covered him with the green turf so that no-one should find him, and sadly stole away.

So ended the earthly life of Robin Hood, hero and outlaw, but his fame will never die, and his spirit lives on in the heart of Sherwood still.